Robert Manners

Pasco

A Cuban tale and other poems

Robert Manners

Pasco
A Cuban tale and other poems

ISBN/EAN: 9783337174699

Printed in Europe, USA, Canada, Australia, Japan

Cover: Foto ©Andreas Hilbeck / pixelio.de

More available books at **www.hansebooks.com**

Pasco,

[A CUBAN TALE,]

AND OTHER POEMS.

BY

R. Rutland Manners.

"Aimer le vrai, le beau ; chercher leur harmonie,
Ecouter dans son choeur l'écho de son génie ;
Chanter, rire, pleurer, sans but, au hasard,
D'un sourire, d'un mot, d'un soupire, d'un regard."
—*De Mussel.*
La Poésie.

PRINTED FOR THE AUTHOR.

CONTENTS.

ODDS AND ENDS:

ERRATA.

INTRODUCTORY NOTE.

In deciding to commit the within collection to *covers*, so far was it from my original intention to present myself as an aspirant for public favor, that I had allowed this Note, as first drafted, to be printed off *in form*, with the statement that I did "not appear in the role of a candidate for public patronage;" explaining therein that I had caused my poems to be placed in this form, as a "matter of gratification to those of my friends, who had 'solicited' me so to do,"— and to myself.

Having determined to appear for judgment, may I here have leave to state, as a consideration to be borne in mind by those into whose hands this little volume may fall, that its contents are the production of the spare hours which have remained to me, from day to day, *after business duties*, for under these most unfavorable circumstances have they, indeed, *all* been written.

While, as has been said, *"a book, to the reader, be not worse or better for the circumstances under which its author has produced it," I would humbly submit, to continue to quote the same learned Writer, that "to rightly estimate any man's performance, it must be compared with his own particular opportunities, * * * to know how much is to be ascribed to native ability and how much to adventitious help." It is in this latter view, that I presume to advance the above palliative; and I cannot but feel that it is only necessary for me to plead a disad-

---

* Dr. Johnson.

vantage so superlatively great, to have a liberal allowance made therefor. While I do not hesitate to state that it is with no ordinary degree of solicitude that I thus venture to intrude myself upon public notice, I am not without hope of success. To confess this, were to admit that I had offered the public that which I knew to be worthless. Should I fail, however, the consciousness that I have lost in an undertaking, pursued under every conceivable disadvantage, will deprive disappointment of its sting.

In varying the order of the rhyme, in the opening poem, from the couplet and alternate to the quatrain,—and in one or two instances becoming an absolute "apostate from poetic rule" by breaking the line short, I have done so to avoid that monotony which results from too close an adherence to any one form, changing the versification from the heroic to octosyllabic, etc., as the respective styles seemed best adapted to the different shadings of the narrative.

As to originality, while I have not knowingly reproduced the thought of another without acknowledging the same, I cannot flatter myself that the one or two instances where I *do* thus credit an appropriated thought, are the only cases where my lines reflect ideas original in others.

Thus do I commit my cause to those before whom I here bring myself to judgment, feeling assured that whatever merit my lines may possess will be liberally allowed.

PASCO.

[A CUBAN TALE.]

Blue roll the waves that lave the southern isles
And crested fall along their coral strands,
Beneath a sky where endless summer smiles
And wreathes in blossoms those celestial lands.
The orange there in rich luxuriance spread
Their yellow wealth along the palm-girt plains
With which the citron-blooms and jessamines*
Upon the air their sweet aromas shed.
And there the sun illumes the bluest sky
That e'er was mirrored in the glassy sea,
Edging with tints of pink transparency
Those waves that lisp their languid minstrelsy
To slumbering shells, which murmur in their sleep,
Soothed by the whispers of the fondling deep.
And from those shores in sullen grandeur rise
Unmeasured heights of pathless mountain steep,
Rearing their heads majestic towards the skies,
As in the clouds their hoary summits sleep,
—While with the bridal of the virgin sky

---

* As is well known, the fragrance of the *Jasmine* species, particularly in
the tropics, is preëminently noticeable above that of all other odoriferous
vegetation of the smaller growths.   M

Their brows are veiled in violet drapery.
From on those heights the native mountaineer
Surveys the waters of th' encircling sea :
Alone his love their rugged steeps to dare,
Nor deems he else an equal luxury,
Though 'neath his view eternal shades abound,
And fruits delicious freight the hidden ground.
As folded flowers in tranquil slumber rest,
On the still air of summer's sultry day,
So sleep those isles upon the placid breast
Of southern seas, where spicy breezes play.
Soft are those winds, with odorous sweets imbued,
Of lemon flowers and rich acacia blooms,
And countless flow rs that breathe their chaste perfumes
Upon the air, by amorous breezes wooed.
Amid the verdure of the islands' shades
Unceasing pour the joyous warblers' song
By gurgling rills and in the flowery meads.
Where o'er bright pebbles streams pactolian throng,
And waving osiers breathe æolian song,
Till o'er cascades where bends the curling vine
They hang the rocks with ribboned crystaline,
Then babble on with smiles for every blade
And every blossom which adorns the glade.
So there the moon's sublimest light illumes
   The sylvan streams which glass her brilliancy.
As 'mid their shades the nightingale consumes
   The tropic eve in languid minstrelsy,
Till the sweet voices of the twilight cease,
And nature's pulses tremble into peace,
When in sweet numbers, to the soft guitars',
Love breathes its story to the list'ning stars.

Entrancing scenes of artless luxury
   Where in profusion lavish nature shed
Her richest stores, nor deem e'en heaven can be
   More fair. its fields more fit for angels' tread.

I I.

The morn across the Antillean seas
Broke softly with a freshing breeze,
Which o'er the bounding billows·swept,
Till in the island groves it slept,
Or wandered merrily along
Amid its shades, which at its song
Waking, their "leafy banners"* hung
Out as it passed, while sweetly sang
The plumaged throng in bright array,
Their anthem to returning day.
To shade and waves the zephyr breathed
Its greeting, and their bosoms wreathed
In smiles,—they all rejoiced to press
The balminess of that caress.
As rippling on in merry glee
In such delightful company,
Till on the shore they sighed to tell
In parting there their sad farewell.
The sun, now risen through the verdant trees,
Tuned by the breeze to rustic symphonies,
Shed o'er * * * Lake, whose waters lay
Within the soundings of Carribea's sea,
It softest rays yet brightest, till its breast
Sparkled with brilliants, like some beauty dressed

---

* Longfellow.

In jeweled splendor, as it rose and fell
In warm pulsation.
                    Here long alone,
Save with his child, scarce to his household known,
Beside these shores had dwelt and slept—now dead—
The *Don Goncalo.* Many years had fled
Since first he sought these shades which now watched o'er
His marble crypt upon the further shore.
Whence he had come none knew;—none e'er had known ;
Why thus he lived, avoiding e'en his own.
And none remembered since the earliest day
He trod those shores one from them spent away.
Though at each eve this man of mystery
Far into night had wandered by the sea,
And only there was he e'er known to show
Aught of emotion ; then, from some deep woe,
It seemed to rise, which in his heart lay sealed,—
Some wearing, secret jealousy concealed.
Stern was his glance, withal yet kind his eye.
Where pride enthroned maintained a mastery
O'er those emotions which his heart downweighed ;
Nor rose unguarded, save when sleep betrayed.
In life, his thought ne'er wearying, did employ
Itself in studying but his daughter's joy ;
And wealth attending left naught to desire,
Save to reclaim from that dark shade her sire :
—Was it remorse or sorrow which thus moved
The heart her own, so truly—fondly loved.
But death, that presence which man's heart subdues,
—Refusing oft' that which alone it sues
In its last hour :—A moment's strength to bear
Up from its tomb the sins pride buries there,—

Had sought *Goncalo* and its fell decree
Forever sealed his life's strange mystery,
Save that unconscious then, his tongue betrayed
Accents that told of passion's hand unstayed
Named with his wife, as wild emotion pressed
Its rending billows o'er his troubled breast:
—She whom those lips had never named before
For years—a stranger to the child she bore.
Now years had fled—to womanhood had grown
The child, yet had she not been left alone
For a not less than mother's love was hers
In one her guardian from her earliest years.

I I I.

Upon * * * lake smooth glidlng o'er
Its waves a gondola approached the shore,
Beneath the oar of swarthy Islander
Borne gently onward.   Long his raven hair
Fell from beneath a ribboned sombrero,
About his neck uncovered—and below,
Across his half bared breast of olive hue,
Floated before the breeze.   His eyes—but who
Would paint a Criollo and shade his eyes
Less dark then are his southern starlit skies
A lovely figure in the bark reclined :
Goncalo's daughter, her sweet form confined
In softest folds of chaste illusion lay,
The very *soul* of grace and symmetry,
Beneath a silk o'ershading, on a spread
Of persian tapestry.   Rested her head

On her warm hand, round which her wealth of hair,
Uplooped with rosebuds, twined and naively there
Their crimson blossoms clung, and seemed to seek
To shade the damask softness of her cheek.
Hey eyes were dark—'twould be a mockery
To try to paint them by a simile,
As they beneath their silken fringe half closed,
In lustrous languor dreamingly reposed.
And, as the moon along the summer sky
Floats calmly on in silvery drapery
Of fleecy clouds—rent by the wind, concealed
Its beauteous form, yet modestly revealed :
So her loose garment by the wind caressed,
Disclosed the beauteous softness of her breast,
Which has pulsating 'neath its folds suggested
A little *snowdrift* with a soul invested.
A terraced stair, with marble balustrade,
Rose from the lake—and thence an avenue,
'Neath palms o'er-arching stretched up the hillside
To where, crowning its summit, the chateau
In antique beauty stood.—Around the shade
Of the mimosa and acacia swayed
In wandering winds laden with sweet distilled
· From neighboring lemon groves, while clustering there
Bloomed floral hues unnumbered, and the air
Amid the foliage musical was filled
                With songs of birds.
Delightful scenes stretched round on every hand
Far as the sight the vista could command,
Of orange groves waving their golden yield
Where royal magnolias ranged the freighted field,

And undulating plains, which to the view
Their stately palms displayed in richest hue,
From which, far distant, rose against the sky
A mountain range in sullen majesty,
Stretching far eastward with the boundless sea :—
The sister tenants of immensity !
            'Neath a mimosa shade,
Amid the verdure with bright blossoms spread,
Where over-arching vines with blooms o'er run,
Tempered the brightness of a tropic sun,
Reclined the figure of a youth, though grown
To manhood's stature. Through the screen o'er thrown
Of foliage intertwined the sunlight crept,
Bathing his brow,—as motionles he slept,
O'er which his hair in indolent unrest
Moved in dark clusters, by the wind caressed.
A flush was warmly glowing on his check
As soft as are the roseate tints that streak
The summer sky when, as night's curtains close
On twilight's breast, day sinks into repose.
So o'er his lips, which closed though not compressed,
Like the wrought marble, changelessly at rest,
The glow of youth in ruddy freshness strayed
As living streams the quiet wood pervade
And there was stamped upon that noble face
Unbending pride, yet tempered with a grace
Of true nobility,—that influence
Which moulds the face in gentler lineaments.
Plain were his features, yet enthroned there,
In native grace, appeared that nameless air
Of conscious force,—the reflex of a mind,
Which still attracts as it commands mankind ;

The superscription of that power which sways
The world, the mind,—that prince of sovereignties !
With its great premier governing reason throned,
Controlling worlds, yet by no power bound.
Its consort thought; the eye its minister ;
The universe its realm ; the arbiter
In man of *men*, who, envious, *then* behold
Themselves resistless by its power controlled,
As in submission, 'neath that master spell,
They render homage, though their wills rebel.

IV.

From midnight till the star of morn
Paled 'neath the saffron veil of dawn,
Young Pasco, o'er the star-lit wave,
By many a cape and island cave,
Full many a league along the shore.
Guided his bark with steady oar
From where, within a cliff-bound bay,
A band of Cuban patriots lay,
Close 'neath the friendly mountain wall
Which stretched around, impassable.
His rich reward fair Lulu's smiles—
His love—the " beauty of the isles."
There in the fastness of the mountain height,
Dreading naught else save the betraying night,
His patriot comrades waited for the day
When once again their hands should rend away
Another thong which bound their bleeding land,
Wrenched from her heartstrings by a tyrant's hand.

*   *   *   *   *   *   *

Thou guardian genius of the patriot brave !
Hear thou thy sons,—stlll thine the power to save,—
Who to thee turn, scourged in their parent land
For freedom's cause, by the usurper's* hand ;
Strike from ambition's grasp the wreaking blade
And kindling brand by blind oppression swayed,
Which o'er that isle, where all's so wondrous fair,
Spreads blackened desolation and despair ;
Hear thou thy sons, who nobly still defy
Thy deadliest foe,—freedom's arch enemy.
Those, chief of despots, whose dark history reads
But a long record of oppression's deeds ;
To thraldom born, that would with envy blind,
Behold their shackles fettering all mankind,
As now, invading that all-sunny clime,
They there would make e'en *liberty* a crime,—
That gift divine, hereditary right,
From mankind stolen in oppression's night.
Thou stricken isle ! how long shall tyrants flood
Thy vales of beauty with the patriots' blood;
How long, still struggling, must thou bleed, nor find
One hand of mercy thy red wounds to bind ?
Weakest, yet braver than the strongest all,
Must freedom's fairest child unheeded call ;
Nor to her sisters in her anguished cry,
Gain but the *echo* of its agony.

    See in yon vale, where Nature's lavish hand
    Spreads rich luxuriance o'er a smiling land ;
    Amid the verdure of his native shades,
    Where sparkling brooklets babble through the glades,

---

   * Usurper, not, perhaps, as having deposed a former acknowledged
sovereignty, but as invading the b:rtbrights of free-born men

The bleeding stag, just staggering to his feet,
In stout defiance meets the tiger's hate,
From whose red jaws on flowery spreads descends
The gouts of scarlet which its fury rends
From those poor limbs, that know no soothing flood,
Save the hot current of their own life-blood.
Thus thou, fair *Cuba ;*—thou *America,*
Freedom's fond mother ; child of liberty !
Thus in thy gates shall stranger robbers slave
The darling offspring which thy throes gave,
—For born of thee she learned thy steps to tread,
And stones ye give her when she asks but bread.
Nay, while her cries now smite thy sluggard rest,
Craving the life blood drawn from thy strong breast ;
While in her flesh, all quivering, deeper gnaw,
Beneath thine eyes, the chains her murderers draw,
Wilt thou, O mother,—*canst* thou, close thy heart
And see the prestige of thy name depart ?
And thou, *Britannia !* foremost *thou to lead*
When justice points where freedom's children bleed :
Whose proud escutcheon on thy strong arm girth
The sun of freedom flashes o'er the earth,
With thy brave offspring,—and as bravely fair—
Let it be thine that glory now to share ;
Liberty's birth, before whose dazzling ray
Tyrants, confounded, shrink in dread away,
As to their lair the preying beasts of night,
When o'er the mountain breaks the morning light.

*   *   *   *   *   *   *   *

Young Pasco, boldest of the brave,
Feared not the wildness of the wave ;
To him the night wind o'er the sea
   Was but a voice of melody ;
Its tossing waves—his heart more free—
   Were but a thing of ecstasy,
In which his boundless thoughts but found
Companions—their impatient sound
Reflecting in their vague unrest,
Love's fevered pulses in his breast ;
And so he welcomed with delight
These restless spirits of the night.
To him—*to none* of they who brave
For woman's love or wind or wave,
Is there a peril which can fright
In trackless seas or mountain height
While still eternities of bliss
Are centered in a woman's kiss.
Now as the dying shades of night
Fled silently before the light
Of coming day, his light caïque
Was moored within an island creek.
Soon reached the scene he knew so well,
Made sacred by the last farewell
Which he had kissed from lips that thrilled
His quick'ning pulse, while parting chilled
His anxious heart ;—as love still dreads
The misty veil the future spreads,
Nor willing yields its sovereignty
To hope, which gilds futurity

With brightness, which its spirit fears
Reflected in a woman's *tears*.
Thus as he now, fatigued, reclined
Beneath a shade, perchance to find
A moment of repose ere day
Should point the hour which should repay
Love's willing toil, his memory drew
The hour of his last adieu,
Which now his heart rejoice to greet :
—Would it not make the joy more sweet
To fold again that form consigned
To hope which ne'er *had* proved unkind?

VI.

As in the loadstone dwells a vital force
We may not trace to its mysterious source,
which seeks its consort, the responding steel,
And to it clings, nor why does it reveal,
Th' effect we mark ;—the *Cause*, there dies the light :
And wonders pauses on the verge of night,
While all the cunning of philosophies
Ends in the simple knowlege that—*it is.*
E'en thus in love a nameless power lies,
Attracting still its own affinities,
Beneath which force the heart responsive moves
Love's willing footsteps toward the thing it loves :
The will obeys,—and *why* it cannot tell,
Yielding unconscious to that mystic spell,
In *spirit*-vision which outwings the sight,
—Pursued by thought in its mysterious flight

Thus oft' there dawns a *seeming* consciousness :
   —Thought's dimmest taper glimmering faint and low,
When near us throbs the heart our own would bless,
   Feeling ere yet its presence we may know :
Still 'tis not *felt*—this intercourse of souls,
   Unknown its workings to the mists of sense,
And yet the will its magic force controlls,
   Which yields unconscious to its influence

Thus as she wandered 'neath the verdant shades
   Which round her island home luxuriant pressed,
As from the lake she sought their quiet glades,
   Dreaming of one whose image filled her breast,
Did Lulu feel this influence which invades
   The realm of thought with pulses to invest
Those cords magnetic which two hearts unite :
—A bond too hallowed for the sensual sight.

And thus impelled, unconsciously she sought
   The floral shade where Pasco sleeping lay.
Wondering the while if life could offer aught
   And Pasco gone ; and then in ecstasy
Transfixed she stood, as quick that saddening thought,
   Darkening her eyes, faded in tears of joy :
—And O how bright beamed those all-lustrous eyes
'Neath that one cloud, flashing love's sympathies.

" My *Pasco*,"—and her voice sank sweetly lower
From the first pulse of love's temerity,
   Like the lone nightingale's, in twilight's hour,
As when disturbed its warblings die away ;
And flushed her cheek as, like an arching flower,
O'er him she leaned in love's expectancy,

Pressing her heart which throbbed all envious,
That sleep should claim a moment of its bliss.

O love, thou sweet enigma of the soul.
  Fearless yet fearful ; all-seeing yet how blind ;
Omniscient yet thou spurn'st the mild control
  Of thy co-dweller *reason*, thus combined
Opposing forces blend a marvellous whole
  In thy mysterious framework,— that designed
By goodness infinite that from its rise
The soul might *glimpse* the fields of paradise.

Pleasures which once no joy could e'er impart,
  Or longings waked they could not satisfy,
'Neath this sweet force find echo in the heart,
  Breathing of its diviner ministry.
Love heaven's rich dower to man of life the part
  All sacred all immortal, which shall be
Eternally as it hath ever been,
The *life* of life,—of life the origin.

Well Lulu spent about the time required
  To read the last two stanzas of my rhyme.
In that impatience which by love inspired
  Makes every breath a century of time.
Fearless, and yet her trembling heart conspired
  To stay the utterance of its joy sublime,
And on her lips, capricious bound the kiss
There waiting restless its approaching bliss.

But love no longer could resist, and now
　　Beside him seated 'mong the flowers, Lulu
One long and lingering kiss upon his brow
　　Impassionately pressed,—then back she drew,
As fearing love too bold, while a warm glow
　　Suffused her cheek ; then o'er his face anew
Her own she leaned, as Pasco, waking, seemed
As if he doubted if he lived or dreamed.

" Is it a dream ?　No, no.　No dream could trace
Such wondrous beauties as my Lulu grace ;
No vision paint an image half so fair
As thou, my idol,—and thou sought me here,
Thou, beauty's self !"　Then in one long embrace,
Upon his breast pillowed her lovely face,
In speechless joy her idoled form he pressed
Close to the heart which trembled in his breast.
" Not *here*, my Pasco—*everywhere* this heart
In spirit flight hath followed where thou wert,
At morn and eve,—and through night's vision still,—
The paths exploring of each neighboring hill,
As hope still promised with each coming day
Thy watched return—how oft' but to betray,
Yet when its voice with less assurance came,
And busy memory ceaseless called thy name,
Love, trembling, sank on sorrow's pallid breast,
And there, disconsol'te, sobbed itself to rest.
But this no more ;—sorrow shall wait on joy,
Which must alone the hours now employ
With thy return, thou truant wanderer ;
And first account thee since we parted here.

Then did thou promise by thine own true heart
E'en thus : ' but for a little time we part ;'
And now the moon, then newborn, hung on high,
Full thrice hath waned along the summer sky.
And see !—why thus in military mien
Art thou returned ?   Where hath my Pasco been,
That thus of dress, as for some carnival,
Absence hath been so strangely prodigal ?
' Tis sure thy humor,—yet thy pensive eye
Scarce seems to bear such presence company."
" Then with thine own softly persuasive eyes,
Shall they but bear love's happier embassies :
E'en as thou say'st : ' *Sorrow on joy shall wait,*'
As love would e'er sorrow anticipate*
Which *still* o'erbodes ; for 'tis but *joy* to weigh
In love's sweet balance sorrows *passed away.*
Called from thy side,—still in our country's cause,—
The cause of freedom and of justice laws,
Employed each hour,—too brief to liberty,
Yet O how lengthened distant far from thee.
Would 't were not mine to tell thee that in vain
Our land still struggles 'neath oppression's chain ;
That still her sons must strive, nor free her soil
From despots who her of her rights despoil.
Come now the hour when all who love their isle,
As hating those who still her vales defile,
Must strike for freedom, nor e'en shrink to bear
Its standard foremost in the ranks of war."
  " Thus hast thou ever nobly born thy part,
    Allegiance sharing but with this fond heart.

---

* Forestall.

My Pasco, till of all thou once possessed—
All save thy *life*, in this art thou divest."
" That gift alone is worthy freedom's cause,
—Her sword reproachful till each patriot draws—
And if but *ventured*—on that hazard cast.
Rich the reward, if that loved cause at last
Triumphant stands ; and if *this* may not be,
Better to die than live for tyranny.
But of thyself" (for still did Pasco fear
To hope and love-expectant to declare
Honor's last sacrifice) " my Lulu, tell
The hour's record, which thou hast marked so well
By the pure moon, which now more chaste must prove,
Since it hath been companion to my love."
Then were recalled those hours of bitterness
When hope beamed low, those "tremblings of distress."*
Which rend the heart when separation flings
Dark chilling shadows from its sombre wings :
Each day remembered with its train of fears ;
Patience grown weary ;—faith subdued to tears,
Till in love's presence all dissolved in light
With beauty beam—love's sweet smiles to invite—
Like those dark mists the risen sun imbues
As breaks the morning, with unnumbered hues.

* * * * * * * *

So sped the hours—so swiftly do they fly
Unmarked by thought in love's sweet company,
Till now they led adown the glowing west,
Beyond the wave, the God of day to rest.
Then, as the clouds which neath the moon's clear light
In beauty drape the majesty of night,

* Byron.

When swept away by spirit winds that sigh
Their weird lamentings through the silent sky,
To *darkness* fade—thus borne from their bright sphere
Into the regions of the nether air;
Shadowing o'er the watching stars but now:
Beaming in beauty on their silvery brow
So the glad light which shone in Pasco's eye
—Reflected from love's fervency of joy,
Now died away as from the shades of thought
Memory recalled that ill in joy forgot;
That dark foreboding which with deep unrest
Disturbed the pulses of his troubled breast,
And threw a shade of sadness o'er his brow
Which beamed so bright with happiness but now:
But quick his heart again forbade that this
Should shadow o'er his star of loveliness,
As it recalled that cloud which thought had thrown
Across his face.—Yet ere 'twas wholly gone
Her upturned eyes then fixed upon his own,
With love's perception marked that shadow fade,
Which to her own his troubled heart betrayed.
Then thus she spoke :—" My Pasco must I trace
One line of sadness falling o'er thy face
Nor know the sorrows which thy heart invade.
And thus the brightness of thine eyes o'er-shade;
Must love with love share naught but *happiness*.
Nor make its own the sorrows that oppress
The heart which yields the only joy it knows;
From which the essence of its being flows.
Nay thus to share thy sorrows but shall be
To add to love a *keener* ecstasy;

Nor deem thy voice one accent e'er can tell
To pain this bosom—lest it be *farewell*,
For still with thee this heart can now no pain,
And welcome sorrow when we part again"
While thus she spoke proud adoration filled
His throbbing heart with quickening pulses thrilled
As in his eyes rose those all holier fires
Which pure affection in the breast inspires,
While thus devotion in her heart displayed
New springs of goodness ne'er before betrayed
From which sweet faith with gracious hand supplied
Entrancing draughts, thus doubly sanctified,
But when of parting *her* loved accents spoke
From his sweet dream of happiness he woke,
And in his heart, as falls a funeral knell,
Choking its pulses *crushed* that word "*farewell.*"
As o'er his face a shade of sadness swept,
And in his eyes their wonted brightness slept,
Which for a moment sought the neighboring sea
In vague unquiet ere he made reply.
Then thus he spoke : " My Lulu couldst thou see
Within my heart its weight of agony
That from thy side a voice all must obey :
Liberty's death-cry summons me away.
Would love dare hide what honor's act hath done
From thee e'en *still* my own my lovely one,
That for thy sake no slightest cloud should lower
To cast one shadow in this longed for hour.
Whence now I come, beset by tyrant hate,
Gathered our comrades for the struggle wait ;
Wait for the hour when Cuba's foes shall know ;
Not unavenged her children's blood shall flow.

For though on freedom treads the oppressor's heel,
Crushing it downward, shall the tryants feel
For them from freedem's bleeding wounds shall flow
A poison deadlier than their hate can know.
Thus have I dared enlist for liberty
The life which love consecrated to thee
At whose command returned to thee I bear
My heart, sweet one, which asks thine own to share
Its sacrifice,—yet fear not hope shall prove
Beauty's sustainer and the strength of love.
The midnight passed unknown the shades of fate,
For thee my heart with longing pulses beat
Whose sweet assurance should impart new life
Te brave the perils of th' impending strife.
Then through 't was death, for thee my loveliness
Scaling the rocks which wall the mountain pass
Where lie our band I sought the neighboring sea
Whose friendly billows bore me safe to thee."
She heard—yet dared not trust her tongue t' impart
The cry of sorrow echoing in her heart,
As motionless she clung to his embrace,—
Save that along her frame her wild distress
A tremor sent, the coldness of despair
Within her heart which now was chilling there,
Beneath which presence trembling fled away,
Fond hope still lingering longingly to stay.
—Hope that still waits e'en where relentless death
From some loved form hath claimed the fleeting breath
Nor yields through darkest fall the mists of gloom
Till at the all inexorable tomb
Palsied with grief it views, *e'en doubting still*,
That cherished form laid in the ' narrow cell '

Then in one pang yields up the life which fe l
Upon the features of its idoled dead.*
"And is it thus ",—that shut within her breast
By sorrow prisoned, her sad accents ceased
As on his breast she sank,—a drooping flower,
Voiceless beneath that grief that hath but power
To *feel*—and in its night of woe to see
But the dark image of its agony.
" Nay let not tears bedim thy lustrous eyes
Nor cloud of sorrow o'er thy beauty rise
For though night lowers it must fade away
—And O what brightness waits returning day.
Before the sunlight melts along the main
Its waves must bear me to our band again,
While hope shall guard love's consecrated shrine,
Which sacred charge to it must love resign."
" To *hope*," she sobbed, "to hope, whose changeful ray
Ever receding, beams but to betray,
While still with light delusive it illumes
The mists of sorrow which it ne'er consumes.
But no," and now in calmer voice she spoke.
Though from her breast its anguished pulses broke
In trembling utterance, " no, our country's need
" Must not unanswered to her children plead,
And shall her daughters from that cup once shrink
Which to its dregs her sons so proudly drink?
Go thou, my Pasco, though each hour shall knell
Its wail of sorrow from this sad farewell.

---

* I must claim indulgence in venturing to insert the preceding eight lines.
The strophe is introduced, *however incongruously*, to portray the *constancy* of
hope,—not certainly as presenting a figure of hopelessness to be attributed to
my subject.

And night returning in each breast shall sigh
The weary reckoning of recurring day,
Till thy return,—O God, should this be not—"
And hope shrank, trembling from that direful thought,
As one wild burst of anguish swept her breast,
And choked its pulses trembling into rest.
Amid the flowers he laid her form,—and now
Brushed the dark tresses from her pallid brow,
And with warm kisses, as o'er her he kneeled,
Sought to restore the life which pain congealed.
And through their channels from her heart to bear
The crowding currents which were chilling there.
A spirit of tenderness sought her sweet face,
Smoothing each line to placid loveliness,
—A beatific calm like that in death
Which still reflects, though ceased fore'er the breath,
The soul's last, *sweetest* smile : that halo shed
O'er th' all *but living features of the dead.*
Then raised her eyelids, fringed in mourning hue,
Where tears were trembling as the early dew
Trembles in beauty 'neath the paling night
Ere well the sun dissolves it into light.
On him, half wondering, fixed her saddened eyes
Where resignation draped love's sympathies,
Which there were gathered, with her sable shade
For hope deep in the heart's sepulchre laid.
As in his arms he raised her to his side,
Around his neck her own were calmly laid,
While that pure tribute love's chaste throbbings yield
Upon his lips in lingering fear was sealed.
　　" Farewall, my Lulu," and his voice betrayed
The deep emotion which his bosom swayed ;

" Farewell ; the morn must to my comrades prove
That Pasco's honor 's stronger than his *love*,
And shame the fear which stings my thought to view
That to his country Pasco was untrue."

   *   *   *   *   *   *   *   *

One kiss—another—

          Now alone she stood
In the drear waste of memory's solitude,
Where hope's sad spirit wailed and echoed o'er,
Chilling life's currents, " here forevermore."

VII.

The moon high o'er *Del Cobre's* sombre height
Dispelled the shades of the unwelcome night,
Flooding the vale and towering mountain side
   In silvery light.   Adown the valley gleamed,
In gracious curves, calm *   *   * wandering tide,
   Till winding 'neath a dark abyss it seemed
To seek repose 'neath the o'er-frowning height,
Whose sombre front repelled the moon's clear light,
As some great serpent drags its weary length
Within the shadows of its cavern strength.
   All motionless, like troops of hadean ghosts,
In groups and isolate, the plain across,
   Ranged the dark palms, which the bright armored hosts
On heaven's battlements watched tremulous.
No sound disturbed the stillness, save the cry
Of the lone night-bird calling plaintively,
With the soft voice communing with the night
Of falling water, white in the moonlight,

Which from the mountain, sought the river's breast,
And with it mingling hushed itself to rest.
Far up the height, along a mountain pass,
Skirting the brink of measureless abyss,
Now and anon gleamed 'gainst the darkened height
Of rock o'ertowering, the portentous light
Of glist'ning steel, whose momentary gleams
Chilled the soft whiteness of the moon's pale beams.
There on the height repose the patriots sought,
Slumbering upon their arms, yet wakeful, caught
The voice which told another hour had gone,
Which cunning *time* from friendly night had won,
As in the mount's defile the sentinel
In cautious utterance said, " men, all is well."
Then quick again upon the pass he stood,
Courting its shades, as the calm solitude
Of vale and pass he watched with jealous care ;—
Ah ! who could dream that death was lurking there ?

*   *   *   *   *   *   *   *

" And dost thou think the rebel watch can sight
From where thou say'st they hold yon mountain height,
The stream below where shades its breadth half o'er
Yon darkening cliff ?   There may the further shore
Alone be reached : too deep the river's bed
Here where concealed these friendly shades o'erspread
To ford its depths ;—and well I deem 'tis meed
If men must die, 'tis nobler that they bleed ;
Then if our foes like they of *Yara's* fight.
None may be spared who strive for *Spain* to-night.
But *there* we cross,—and thou canst lead us on,
As thou hast said, and by a path unknown ? "

" I can, my chief : within a cave it ends,
And thence the path through narrow gorge ascends
To a defile where lie the rebel crew.
The *pass* is sure : the rest an hour must show."
" Well thou hast spoke.   Soldiers," he turning said,
—The dark battalion there beneath the shade
Stood motionless,—

   " The enemies of Spain
Keep yonder height, nor dream ere night shall wane
The rocks that now their rebel slumbers keep
Loud shall re-echo with their own death shriek.
We cross below where yonder rock o'ershades.
Look to your arms ; guard well no naked blades
A warning bear to traitor eyes,—for know
But to their *hearts* such messengers should go."
Then to the guide : " Pepillo, lead the way ;
Now steady—*march !*"   The column moved away
Along the stream, and silently it trod
With measured cadence o'er the yielding sod.
Soon reached the ford, they halted.   " Pepillo,
Scan well the height—say canst thou see the foe ? "
" Look thou, my chief, seest thou that gleam of light—
Wait but a moment- -now upon the height
Above the fall ? "

   " Aye, there—but now 'tis gone.
Lose not a moment"—

   " Steady, men, as one,
March !"   In they moved.   Invaded thus, the stream
Plaintively muttered—as in some strange dream
The restless slumberer.

   —Soon 'twas left to rest,
And scarce a ripple trembled on its breast.

Traversed the plain 'neath the disguising wood,
Soon at the mount the halted column stood.
Once more was scanned with stealthy eyes the height ;
Once more there glimmered that betraying light,
As the clear moon illumined the pass. till now
Veiled by the shadows from the cliff's dark brow.
Beneath the shades which clothed the mountain sides
The chief held whispered council with the guide ;
Then at their head, prepared to lead the band,
He silent waited for the chief's command,
Who at his side in measured whispers said.
While all stood motionless as are the dead :
" Now comrades, softly ; muffle e'en your breath,
Nor let your footsteps prate of coming death.
When reached the cave, by fours close column keep ;
Thence scarce ten paces where the rebels sleep,
Where once again must traitors, bosoms feel
The deadly coldness of the Spaniards' steel."

    *   *   *   *   *   *   *

Along the mountain tops the day
Arrayed in robes of sombre grey,
Crept on apace, as Pasco stood
In turn to guard the solitude
Of the defile and vale below.
Which now the moon—suspended low,
With shadows thronged that lengthened loomed
Along the glen like spirits doomed
To endless silence,—gathering there
With waving plumes, as if to bear
The dying night unseen,—afar,
To its mysterious sepulchre.

Beneath the cooling breath of morn
His comrades, now fatigued and worn
By hours of wearying, restless sleep,
Now lay, o'ercome, in slumber deep,—
Like that which soothes the feeble breast
When fever's crazing pulse is passed,
And motionless composure gives,
With scarce a throb to tell it lives.
Yet wakeful in each weary breast
One thought watched o'er the patriot's rest :
Ah, but for this it had been mad
To trust to slumber all they had
In hope,—from Freedom's beckoning star
Which brightly beamed though distant far :
--That thought their land, which to such hearts
A deathless double life imparts.
An hour had passed, and Pasco stept
Within the pass to where still slept
His comrades, though their eyelids lay
Just bound by sleep's sweet mystery.
He turned the cliff —

            Then forward sprang,
As on the startled silence rang,
Rebounding with a hundred shocks
From peak to peak of towering rocks,
His carbine's crash—the signal set
  Should night unmask her dread alarms,
And they surprised, by foes beset,
  No moment find to *call* to arms--
For springing from a neighboring height,
With bayonets glimmering in the light

Of early dawn, he there beheld
The hated foe,—as wildly swelled
Those phrensying pulses in his breast
Those feel by tyranny opprest,
Which know no wilder throb of hate
Than that when face to face they meet
Their despot's slaves, who crav'n would dare
To bind them with the chains they wear.
Quick as his thought his lead as true,
Struck from the cliff a foeman low ;
Nor had the signal failed, as told
A crash of musketry which rolled,
Re-echoing with the thunder's might
From where the patriots held the height,
'Neath which above the crash arose
The death-shriek of a score of foes,
Which from the patriots brought a cry
Of stern defiant mockery.
Then quick in fierce reply outrang,
As Pasco 'midst his comrades sprang,
A volley from the Spaniard band,
Now closing fast on every hand,
And 'neath its storm of iron hail
Full many a noble patriot fell,
Employing still ere hushed by death
The accents of his latest breath
In freedom's name as to her foes
His shout of proud defiance rose.
As rush the waves' impetuous might
Against the cliff's opposing height,
Their foam-locks streaming in the storm, —
Each like some fierce demoniac form,

On sweeping with resistless force
The strength which seeks to stay their course,
Till backward hurled in turn they lay
Low quivering in their parent sea,
Again to rise—and yet again,
As oft' flung backward to the main,
Yet shivering as they fiercely rush
The tottering height they may not crush :
So now, with bayonets set, and hair
Back floating on the trembling air,
—No time for aught save steel now left,
Forward the island patriots swept,
Led on,—if aught the brave e'er *lead*,
By Pasco waving at their head
Their country's flag, full proud to give
Their lives, that its loved cause might live.
Fired by the madly coursing blood
Which swelled each pulse, a phrensying flood,
Upon the hireling foe they dashed,
Undaunted, though out-belching flashed
Full in their course a withering breath
Of flame, red-tongued, which seethed with death.
Mute as the dead, nor stopped, nor stayed,
With fixed eyes and jaws close laid ;
Each springing where a comrade fell
There summoned by his last death yell,
Breathing that atmosphere of hell.
Onward they swept, like wave on rock,
Till now, with all resistless shock,
Closing upon the foe, they rushed ;
Beneath that shock recoiling, crushed

Down—down—as many a bosom writhed
Beneath the freezing steel there sheathed ;
Yet lingered not, but quick once more
The thirsty metal wreaked in gore,
As with insatiate greed it leaped,
Still dripping scarlet doubly steeped,
From breast to breast, deep curdling there
The currents stagnant 'neath despair,
Till cleft the arm which urged it fell
Low quivering in its purple rill.
High swelled the frightful din of war,
The wild death shreik ; the shivering jar
Of splintering steel ; the stiffled groan,
Half choked ere breathed ; the fitful moan
From life's low pulse ; the sabres' shock
Which rose, down swept—too fiercely lock :
—Nor loosed their hold till rent apart,
Then plunged revengeful in each heart :
—As if imbued with *very life*,
Conscious they shared their masters' strife.
Ah, who that awful shock may tell,
When waves of human anger swell
In fierce contention—battling where
Meet livid hate and grim despair ;
Who paint that hour of phrenzied strife
When passion spares not—*asks* not life ;
Nor deems its warmest, softest breath
As sweet as the cold gasp of death
Forced from that heart where still the steel
It pressed with a savage zeal.
Now backward forced scarce half remain,
— But step by step—then yet again

Fierce dashing on the staggered foe,
Each laid another Spaniard low,
As sinews straining, hand to hand
The few still left of that brave band—
Pale as the dead ; each forehead set
With beads of cold, congealed sweat ;
While from their breasts down-trinkling rolled
The scarlet gouts, or stream that told
The murderous sabres' mission there,
Red-gleaming on the troubled air—
Sprang at a foe defiant still,
In hate which death alone could kill.
Beset as one of wolves the prey,
Full twenty sabres kept at bay,
Back forced, contending *foot* by *foot ;*
Red stained from many a streaming cut,
There Pasco, foremost in the fray,
Battled the foe defiantly.
Above his head the flag he held,
One arm but free its folds to shield,
Which wielded with resistless might
His sabre,—busiest in the fight.
Struck from his hands the colors lay,
Forward he dashed : the foe gave way,
Save one more bold who dared contest
His way, and sought from him to wrest
The prize regained, but all in vain
—One more was numbered with the slain.
Then quick again he waved it o'er,
Its folds now steeped in crimson gore,
As up his height he proudly drew
And fearless scoffed the hated foe.

But the fast ebbing scarlet tide
Down coursing from his breast and side,
Had sapped his life, and that proud cry
Broke in a gasp of agony.
Then on their victim doomed they pressed
—Back staggering, till by deep abyss,
From which up-rose a doleful roar
Like that from waves which beat the shore
Far distant heard, now Pasco stood
Defiant still—still unsubdued,
While round him, eager for his life,
His foes fast closed. The torrent's strife
Deep down the gorge he heard and knew
It swept a thousand feet below,
Nor aught between where hope could trace
For Daring's foot a refuge place.
Then the first fear his bosom knew
Cast o'er his face a pallid hue,
As there now mingling curdled stood
Out-starting drops of sweat and blood.
—One glance quick sought the foe-kept pass ;
Quick one the yawning precipice,
Then with a shout of proud disdain—
A challenge to the arms of Spain—
He turned and down the cañon leaped
—Still grasped the flag so bravely kept ;
So nobly borne in life 'twas meet
In death 't should be his winding sheet.

    *   *   *   *   *   *

The struggle o'er, in death's embrace
Each patriot soldier face to face

There with his foe sank down to rest
—Undrawn the blades from each still breast.
The sunbeams there that morning played
On many a shattered sabre blade,
But warmed not those who ne'er might know
Again its life-exhaling glow.
Still now the scene an hour before
Which echoed with red-battle's roar
And mingling there together flowed
The Patriots' and the Spaniards' blood.
No sign of life was seen save where
The vulture soaring high in air,
Amid the sky's ethereal blue,
Looked down upon the scene below.
As they had fall'n so there they lay
Till time should hide them in decay,
Nor lived one of that band to tell
How Cuba's valiant children fell.

NOTE.—In the second and concluding division of this poem, in following the heroine in her search for her lost lover, I had designed to picture, to the best of my ability, the treatment meted out to and disposition made of "los rebeldes" when captured by the Spaniards,—this more particularly in the fortressed cities of the Western Department of the Island, Santiago de Cuba, Manzanilla, etc., incorporating in my rhyme a recount of some of the more notorious acts of barbarism of Spanish warfare in that the "ever faithful isle;" I say "I had designed :" I have not abandoned this purpose, but feeling that I could not, in justice to the subject,—or to myself, under existing circumstances, undertake to complete the tale, I have determined to *bide* a more "Congenial season."

𝔖pring.

AN IDYL.

"Nature exerting an unwearying power
Forms, opens and gives scent to every flower,
Spreads the fresh verdure of the fields, and leads
The dancing Naiads through the dewy meads."
—*Cowper.*

Hail heavenly goddess with thy floral train !
Nor from thy praises can my muse refrain,
As joining with the blithesome sylphs that throng
Along thy way and wake the earth with song
And merriment, it would thy steps attend
And with their praise its humbler plaudits blend.
It would thy course o'er hill and mead pursue
As these thou deck'st with robes of richest hue
And wreathes of flowerets while the joyous earth
From slumber wakes thy darling offspring Mirth,
Who hand in hand with roguish Jollity
In thy glad train trips on right merrily ;
In flight ethereal o'er thy path he moves
With winged attendants from Idalia's groves,

Twining thy brow with bacchanalian wreathes
And to each nymph the sparkling grape bequeaths;
By Dionysus all hilarious led—
Showers of blossoms falling on his head—
He chases Frolic while the aerial bands
Applaud the effort with rejoicing hands
And hill and dale the glad applause resound
Till song harmonious fills the air around,
As in his arms the victor clasps his prize,
—Buried in laurels where fatigued he lies.

  * * * * * * *

All beauteous Spring! thou darling of the spheres,
Before whose smile shamed Winter disappears,
His face conceals yet lingers to survey
The gladd'ning prospects which thy charms display;
What are thy charms let Nature's self declare
To those who doubting to her courts repair.
Where scenes delighting stretch on every hand
As thou with garlands strew'st the smiling land.
Thy splendor not the dazzling pomp of kings
The Muse adoring all enraptured sings;
Not the vain pageant partial fate bestows
Upon the few to mock the many's woes
Sinking its slaves in luxuries that blind
Till man becomes unfaithful to mankind;
Naught such as this thy liberal hand displays :—
Impartial still, *this* would enjoin my praise
Which gives to all nor circumscribed reveals
The humblest mortal but its bounty feels,
While round the peasant in his mountain cot
Are spread thy gifts where princes are forgot;

Richest profusion decks their mean abodes—
Unknown to man yet favored of the gods—
His humble home delights thy earliest care
While princely state remaining bounties share.
Thy generous hands around the quiet dead
Brightest of flowers with lavish kindness spread
And blossoms ladened there with sweet perfume
Declare thy memory of the silent tomb.
And O how lovely do thy flowers appear
Where all is still—so sweetly quiet there;
There where the cherished of our hearts repose
When life's short day in evening's shadows close,
Where softly bright beneath the cypress bloom
Roses which tint the shadows of the tomb
—Breathing so sweetly on that hallowed air
That peace itself appears enseraphed there,
And modest daisies with chaste violets wed
Their fitting emblems o'er the slumbering dead
While humbly o'er immortal amaranths wave,
Telling of life which lies beyond the grave.
So when not ours to speak that last farewell
Which in death's hour the bursting heart would tell;
To catch the accents of that fleeting breath
Which all composed resigns itself to death,
How sweetly do these emblems of the dead
Commune with us of those whose souls are fled
And to the heart a silent rapture give
Through memory's voices which forever live.
But still the glories of thy work I sing,
O ever beauteous,—ever friendly Spring;
Amid thy scenes delighted still I stray.
As thou with flowers adorn'st the smiling day,

And love to mark each change that charms the view
Which o'er the fields thy lithesome steps pursue.
See in the meads streams carol as they run
O'er pebbles colored golden by the sun
Where meek-faced violets from retirement look,
Bathing their leaflets in the passing brook,
And yellow cowslips flaunt their gaudy dress
Trailing their skirts o'er spreads of velvet cress,
While everywhere throughout the landscape sway
In balmy winds the "darling buds of May."
Thus on the mountain side the forests bare
Become the objects of thy tender care,
Outward to thee stretching their naked arms
Rejoiced t' embrace thy all-delightful charms,
And these adorned bedeck the bleak ascent,
—Of thy great work the grandest monument!

   *   *   *   *   *   *   *

When the soft morn for flight her pinions spread,
Moving with blushes from her saffron bed,
As the blue arch which props the eastern sky
Her rosey wings with softest tint supply;
When the first beams of the approaching day
Across the landscape take their quiet way
—In that still hour which contemplation loves,
As nature thus from calmest slumber moves—
How sweet to wander through the smiling fields
And breathe the fragrance nature's garden yields,
Where every bud which decks the verdant space
In due degree fills its appointed place,
And in each flower some differing beauties lie
While *all* their Maker's handiwork display;

How sweet to rest 'neath some sequestered shade
By passing zephyrs in their wanderings swayed
And contemplate vast nature's boundless scheme,
Supreme creation of a Power supreme !
On every hand some lesson man may learn ;
In every flower some hidden truths discern :
View with the rose attending thorns appear
And sharpest thorns the sweetest blossoms bear ;
Mark the meek violet and the giant tree
Share his regard in their required degree—
All eloquent, bespeak their God's defence
And show to man impartial providence.
Here warbling songsters fill the verdant shades
And streamlets sparkle through the flowery glades
Which, with soft winds that tune the whispering trees
Flood the bright scene with rapturing symphonies,
High the lark warbles o'er the murmuring trees
And hurrying swallows skim adown the breeze,
While the glad lapwing as she upward springs
Flashes the sunlight from her busy wings.
The faithful red-breast, first of all the year,
Sings to its mate in numbers softly clear
And gives good morrow to the whistling thrush
Which greets the songster from a neighboring bush ;
While Zephyrus her fragrant breezes lends
As with the warblers her soft chorus blends,
—The aerial gathering decked in varied coats
Swelling the anthem with their mellow notes,
Till crowning all in the festivous scene
Heaven's royal gold weds Earth's imperial green,
From which great union spring in glorious birth
Unnumbered flowers which deck their mother earth

At which all nature in grand concert sings
And all the plumaged concourse clap their wings.

     *   *   *   *   *   *   *

The Occident now dons her saffron dress
Its orange flounces edged with violet lace,
The royal sun approaching with the eve
In her enchanted palace to receive.
Ablaze with light its grand dimensions stand
Out 'gainst the heavens which above expand,
—The arching battlements with crimson hung
And fleecy banners from their summits flung,
Tinted with purple and enfringed with gold   .
Which to the heavens their wavy lengths unfold
As 'neath the portals moves the god of day
Followed by the celestial pageantry,
As waiting Nox swings to the gates of light
And shuts the scene majestic from the sight,
When gathering fast attend the sentrying stars
Marshaled by their proud queen and chieftain Mars.
The lowing herd now homeward takes its way—
Each drowsy member following o'er the lea—
As the weird spirits of the dying light
Attend in silence the approaching night.
Hushed nature sleeps cradled in verdant bowers
On softest beds of fragrant breathing flowers,
As day upon the bosom of twilight
Slumbers,—and Cynthia reigns the queen of night,
While darkness o'er the sky her covering lays
Fastened with brilliants from the pleiades.
Now in the wood sings modest philomel
Her notes nectareous on the stillness swell,

As willing Echo, waking at the strain,
Replies harmonious to the pure refrain,
In shaded haunts where Cynthia's soft beams glide
'Mid slumbering leaves reposing side by side
To woo the brooklet which with dimpled smile
Their love indulges the hours to beguile.
But ever fickle now in truant glee
She scampers off, babbling coquetishly,
To Sylva's side who waits her darling choice
And breathless listens for the well loved voice.
—Soon dewy showers disturb the vesper lay
And philomela's warblings die away,
While echo with her sinks into repose
And silence o'er the earth her mantle throws.

Monody

On the Death of the unfortunate poet Thos. Chatterton.

———

"That marvelous boy that perished in his pride."
— *Wordsworth.*

———

Inspire O Muse ! the sadd'ning theme I raise
To one who loved thy presence, sang thy praise
In sweetest voice of all thy minstrel choir
From the first hour his fingers swept the lyre
Received from thee,—its dulcet strings supplied
From silver in that fire purified
Which on the altar of thy temple still
Lives, though now smouldering, on thy sacred hill.
Inspire my theme ; a theme adorned to grace
Thy sweetest songs ; the noblest minstrel's lays,
To him whose lyre,—so rich its numbers came—
Shed a new glory on thy sacred name ;
A heaven-born spirit which from its bright sphere
Wandering to earth lingered a little here
To sing the songs which it had known before
With kindred spirits on the Elysian shore,

—Earth's tongue in their diviner harmonies
Echoing here the music of the skies.
Sweet bard! how bright thy sun of promise rose
Yet O what shadows gathered to the close,
And ere it reached the height of life's noon-day
In mists of darkness quenched fore'er its ray:
How bright that sun, behold where passed its light
A star of glory illumines death's night,
Yielding a beam immortal to that fire
Which on fame's height lights genius' sacred pyre!
Amid the quiet of thy native woods,
Where the sweet voices of its solitudes
Contentment breathed, the brook, the meek-faced flower
The grateful songster; and in night's still hour,
The stars were thy sweet loves still sought by thee
With more than fondest lover's constancy,
Drawn to their chasteness by that force which gives
To love to seek its own correlatives.
Thy faithful heart, e'en as the creeping vine
Struck by the worm, around its loved did twine
Its greenest offerings, yielding sweetest breath
E'en while below cankered the worm of death:
Thy love its rich warm soil; its only air
Draughts humid with the cold mists of despair;
Its only light hope's distant dying ray
A spark expiring—in eternal day.
Relentless fate, inexplicable doom!
Which thus consigned thy genius to the tomb
And swept thy hopes, thy promise richly fair
Into the grave to sleep forever there;
Nor let thee know in life's resigning breath
The kindred voice that soothes the pain of death.

Then in thy mind bright scenes forever past
Upon thy soul distracting shadows cast
To make thy agony but deeper grow
Till thou hadst supped the very dregs of woe,
While—as the lightning's momentary flight
Illumes the clouds encumbering the night
And breaks the darkness of the midnight sky
But to increase its black intensity—
Memories of home within thy hapless breast
Flashed through despair's thick cloud that round thee pressed,
Which in their brightness served but to illume
How dark the gathering shadows of the tomb
And, passed away, in thy distracted mind
Left a thick darkness doubly black behind.
As lesser spheres a symmetry do show
As truly perfect as the greater, so
The narrowed circle of thy life not less
Perfection showéd for its littleness,
Where, like the planet with its belt of light,
Thy star of genius blazed along the height
Of Fame, and, meteor-like, though soon 'twas gone,
Gave forth a glory which was all its own.
Of all mankind the muse did e'er endow
'Twas thine alone mature in youth to know
The "gift divine,"* wherein thou didst display
—An inspiration but revealed in thee—
With genius knowledge; knowledge e'en earth's Seers
Amazed beheld—in all the work of years.

---

* "In our judgment of him" (Chatterton) "age cannot be taken into account; he never seems to have been young. His intellect was born *fully matured*."—ENCY.

With the eternal hills; the great, deep sea
Familiar didst thou commune,—they to thee
Were but as loved companions; with dread voice
The Tempest, robed in night, earth, sea and skies
Stirring to strife, as through the trembling air
Hurling its bolts it swept, its course the glare
Of the fierce lightnings 'luming, was to thee
A sight which gave thy soul supremacy
Of joy, as, with the Storm-king's awful form
Attendant, rode thy spirit on the storm.
Insatiate Pride beneath thy direful sway,
Thou scourge of earth, thou subtle votary
Of death! of genius all thou may'st o'ercome
How oft' hath sought the silence of the tomb;
Youth- beauty, worth, earth's mightiest thy prey;
O'erthrown by thee see nations in decay,
Of which thou 'st left—of Genius, nations, all—
But monuments to show how great their fall.
Serpent-like coiled within that hapless breast
Implacable! 'twas thou his life oppressed;
With lying tongue on to destruction, stilled
The voice of reason, thou his steps beguiled,
Then, e'en when most thou promised, didst betray
To death the victim of thy treachery.
And thou, O world! in thy cold selfishness
Witnessed the victim fall yet to distress,
Born e'en that thou might'st hidden beauties know,
Brought not relief; nay, dealt the final blow
Which all of genius death hath power to bind
To the dark precincts of the tomb consigned.
Is it for this the muse her riches gives;
Is it for this that patient Genius strives,

Earth's hidden things of beauty to reveal
From secret places gleaned with tireless zeal,
—To live the drudge of penury and care;
The dupe of hope; the victim of despair;
The world's cold incredulity to brave;
To sink forgotten to a timeless grave—
That those may share a wealth which else must lie
Buried in Nature's dread infinity,
Who while they scruple not the fruits t' enjoy
Ungrateful coldly pass the laborer by,
Or turn away by envy rendered blind
—That miscreant which to baseness sinks the mind!
May shame smite thee, O selfishness! when on
The tomb that holds the dust of Chatterton
Thou look'st; thou *Pride* and *Envy* should *ye* too
There stray, ye shall shame's deepest lashes know,
While humbled ye within your hearts confess,
Else dumb, how *less* ye are than littleness.

Retrospection.

 LIKE the window open
              with the shading eglantine
Breathing incense with the fragrant
              mignonnette's its leaves enshrine ;
I'll draw the blind a little
              to keep out the setting sun—
There : now I want to hear you play
              my air when you have done.
I mean that plaintive melody
              —you know what I would say—
You played it for me long ago
              as died the light away
That summer's eve when last we met,
              it seems but yesternight,
And though clouds shade remembrance now
              it edges them with light.
The soft *Andante* breathes to me
              of Saint Celia's bells
Borne by the evening breezes
              from the Cloister's wooded hills,

As blending with the murmur
   of the ocean's sad refrain,
And wakes a sweet sad feeling
   intermingling joy and pain,
—Throbbings of joy which sweetly thrill
   by busy memory brought,
Then sadly tremble into rest,
   struck by the chill of thought.
I cannot else explain it
   but that memories of the past
Which that loved melody awakes
   now light now shadows cast
Upon my heart, as its sweet chords
   recall each cherished scene
Which now—sweet pictures of the past!
   but show what " might have been,"
And these alone remain to me
   of all that happy time—
In the soul's darkened chambers hung
   in sad memoriam.
There might have been no shadows :
   do you think I never guessed
The secret hidden in the heart
   now beating in your breast ;
The *would-be* secret from that night
   I left you for the sea
When your dear lips revealed that love
   your tongue withheld from me,
As round my neck your arms were placed
   —I feel their impress yet
For it woke a rapture in my heart
   I never can forget,

And in its depths your eyes kindled
          a fire still smouldering there
Though, like watch-lamps in selpulchres,
          it burns in lifeless air.
You surely loved me, May, but then
          ere wealth was mine—the prize
I sought to gain the *greater*—
          you feared the sacrifice,
For you could not renounce for me
          what I could not supply :
That luxury which you enjoyed
          and could not well deny
Yourself.   For this I blame you not—
          man has no right to claim
Such sacrifice from woman,—
          though they make them all the same,
And though now fortune has removed
          that barrier aside
What matters it since I have lost
          the only wealth I pride.
No, not for this I blame you
          but that when the charm dissolved
Ere it had well been woven,
          that your will again involved
My love.   Ah, you remember it
          for though you answer not
That tear now trembling on your cheek
          shows that the springs of thought
Have been disturbed by memory,
          and thus overflowing rise—
And what a lovely channel
          have they chosen in your eyes.

But take my arm and let us stroll
                along the *lilac-way*,
This may be the last meeting
                we may know for many a day
For I go from here to-morrow,
                I can scarcely tell you where,
I do not know which way myself—
                in truth I little care,
But I dare no longer trust my heart
                by its surrendered shrine
Lest it should seek to repossess
                that which it must resign ;
And I would not between you come,
                you now are his, and so
'Tis better for forgetfulness—for *all*,
                that I should go.
This month you marry him
                —of all the brightest of the year
Which must with each summer's return
                its shade of sadness bear
Hereafter, for 'twill wake the love
                I now must bury in
My heart here where it first was born :
                would that it had not been,
For better far that ne'er had bloomed
                the flower affection gave
Than to have blossomed but to deck,
                as now, affection's grave.
It was beside this gate I stood,
                as you already know,
And heard you play that melody
                which I now cherish so.

The day I met you,—then my love
    woke to that sweet refrain
As its harmony with silver chords
    wove round my heart a chain,
Which though 'tis rent asunder,
    recollection now displays
Its scattered links which still reflect
    the scenes of happier days ;
And with it came an image
    then enshrined within my heart
Where it must rest until the grave
    shall claim it as its part.
But May farewell : I'll leave you now,
    we've parted often here
And this may make it easier
    for both of us to bear—
Or shall I see you to the porch ?
    —it may be wiser so
For your hand is trembling—though perhaps
    'tis better finished now,
And so good-bye : the agony
    which now my heart endured
I pray God with this last adieu
    may never once be yours.

 * * * * * * * *

There is a quiet spirit in the trees
    that shade the dead
Beneath which now I'm sitting
    after many years are fled ;
Tis June again and from her grave
    I'm looking out to sea

From the village church-yard where she sleeps
                    who was so dear to me.
The waves break sadly, as I've heard them break
                    in many a clime,—
Like memories which forever fall
                    along the shores of time—
And the droning bee hums idly by
                    in the drowsy Summer air
Lingering to sip from new-blown sweets
                    which blossom everywhere.
White-winged, a solitary ship
                    far out upon the sea
Reflects the noon-day sunlight
                    —soon o'erclouded, and to me
This seems a fitting image
                    of the lot I bear this day :
Alone on life's broad ocean
                    and the sunlight passed away ;
And o'er its havenless expanse
                    my bark of life must bear
O'ershadowed by those memories
                    which must ever darken there.
Thus hope's delusive star how oft'
                    in sorrow's night declines
And to dark disappointment's shades
                    our happiness consigns ;
Yet can the image which awoke that
                    hope e'er die away
Embalmed in the heart's sepulchre from
                    " feeling's dull decay."

A DREAM.

—

One Summer's day, beside the murmuring sea,
Stretched on the beach, I slept, and dreamed I saw
A noble Ship which, out upon the deep,
Moved proudly o'er the waters toward the east.
Calm as a mountain lake the Ocean spread
Beneath the brightness of a noon-day sun,
Yet it did seem as if the sultry air
Of Summer's heated hour upon its breast
Oppressive lay, and in its mighty heart,
Deep down, disturbed its slumbering forces,—stirred
To restless throbbings, as its bosom swelled
In slow pulsation, and then sank away
In strange disquietude. Encircling, arched
Sublimely o'er the azure vault of Heaven,
Upon whose royal height enthroned sat
The God of day, in dazzling glory robed.
O'er the still depths the Ship majestic moved,
As sportively she scattered with her prow,
About her path—all glittering in the sun,
Unnumbered brilliants of unnumbered hues
Which she did gather from the emerald deep,
While from her rolled upon the drowsy air
A long dark line of smoke, which sought the haze

Of roseate tint, far in the glimmering distance.
Upon her decks the " toilers of the sea,"
Sun-browned in service, each his duty sought
While in the rigging some the useless sail
With busy fingers folded to the yards,
All merry hearted singing as they wrought.
Beneath an awning shading from the sun
Reclined the ocean voyagers, and there
Upon the air all merrily arose
The careless laugh—the voice of happiness,
And busy tongues of little ones at play.
Beauty and youth with faces bright, illumined
With love and hope, and Age with its sweet smile
In happiest intercourse assembled were.
Others apart from those thus grouped about
Sought to beguile in quicker pace away,
The lingering hours of the hot Summer's day
With tales of Fancy's painting ; some o'ercome
By its soporous breath in slumber lay,
While here and there one o'er the bulwarks leaned
In listless dreamings gazing o'er the wave.
Aside were two : one Beauty's prototype
Set in a frame of fairest loveliness ;
The other Beauty's proud defender—Youth
From nature's statelier, bolder model, *Man.*
As silvery clouds in fleecy softness veil
The chasteness of the virgin Summer moon,
Her white attire in sweet abandon draped
Her lovely form—in nameless grace composed,
As she, reclined beside him whom she loved,
Gave ear attent as he read to her thought ;
Read of some sorrow, as expression told,

Moulding her face to sweet solicitude—
Of holy sympathy, throned in the heart,
The superscription.   So her lustrous eyes,—
Liquidly brilliant as the glist'ning dew
Upon the newblown, trembling violet,—
Pearled in warm tears, did each emotion glass
Which that sad tale awoke within her heart.
—Perchance it traced love's fair, young life betrayed,
Blighted by dire deceit, that worm which gnaws,
With venomed fang, the heart whose warmth it gains
Lurked in love's flower, by falseness planted there.
But this was passed and like the Sun's fresh glow
Of heat and light when April showers are o'er,
With a soft brightness beamed her tear-damped eyes,
Resting on him who, ceased, in their sweet depths
Poured from his own love's warm responsive rays.

    *   *   *   *   *   *   *

The scene was changed : upon a rock-bound coast
I stood, darkness had gathered over all.
'Gainst the dark sea high loomed the walling cliffs
Amid the star-lit air, their towering fronts
Stern frowning, om'nous, Warders of the Deep,
Robed in the sombre livery of night.
About their caverned base lamentingly,
The troubled waters tossed, 'neath the weird wind
Which to the night distressfully complained,
In wild and fitful gusts.   Higher it rose
And 'neath it soon high-swelled and fiercely lashed
The surge in angry clamor 'gainst the cliffs,
While black impenetrable clouds rolled o'er,
Piled mass on mass, high 'mid the thickening air,
And quickly curtained with their darkened folds

The ebon vault of Heaven, whose paling lights
Now in their misty caverns disappeared.
Far distant, from its cloud-built battlement,
Rending night's pall, the wakened Lightning pierced
With gleaming shaft the bosom of the Deep.
Responsive to the Storm-kings awful voice,
Deep-swelling from afar, then opened fast
The many portals of the walling clouds,
Piled up the empyrean height, to passage give
The spirits of the tempest.   Issuing forth
They, riding on the winds, did fiercely urge
The elemental strife, most clamorous
Where, lightning led, they ranged the watery waste,
Which, thus illumed, its waves dark, serpertine
Revealed high surging in encounter wild,
Like huge Leviathans in fury met
Fiercely contending.   Now above the roar
Of the loud Sea the deepening thunder rose—
And died away upon the wind, then quick
From the dark zenith of the firmament,
In louder voice its angry mutterings broke,
And rolling downward burst into a crash.
Then every cloud, in emulation fierce,
Thundered reply, rending the trembling air,
As through the ambient darkness, inky grown,
Each gave defiant challenge to the Night,
And hushed the mighty roaring of the sea.
Flaming the lightnings red-tongued licked the waves,
Which heavenward madly reared their mammoth forms,
Till by the Tempest struck back hurled they plunged
With roars defiant to their surging depths.
Out on the sea, lit by the lightnings' glare,

—Flash following flash in wild velocity,
A ship swept on before the Tempest's strength,
Rose with the maddened waves, sank as they sank,
Then in the hadean darkness disappeared.

* * * * * * *

The fulmines of the storm were spent, though still
The forces of the wind swept to the cliffs,
Resistless in their might, hurling the waves,
To fury lashed, 'gainst their black adamant,
As if back summoned to their cavern strengths,
Rebellious they in fierce resentment raged.
The broken clouds now hurried o'er the sky,
And laid their shattered masses 'neath the arch,
Which props the southern limits of the heavens,
Their ragged summits by the moon illumined,
Which now released, in mellow brilliancy
Flooded the waves—to very mountains grown.
There laboring o'er their heights the doomed ship
Rose, mastless, tottered on their giant crests,
Then headlong plunged to their abysmal depths
But rose not up again—the waves rolled o'er
Inexorable. * * * *
From my sleep I woke ;
Still murmuring in the sunset lay the sea.

SONNETS.

The Crucifixion.

———

When on the cross hung man's great Sacrifice
   Death near approached his work to execute,
   Awe-struck recoiled, in fear irresolute
His office on his king to exercise.
Then, bowing to his breast his head, the Christ
   Made sign to the Implacable that he,
   Without regard to right of sovereignty,
Should claim the sacrifice at which was pric'd
Man's sin. *Then* did th' Inexorable strike—
   The fearful sun to darkness paling fled;
   Earth trembling shrank to night's embrace; the Dead,
E'en by that deed of their dread Prince made quick,
Did him defy—he had forever spent
   His power in striking the Omnipotent.

My Mother.

Remember thee, my mother ! While this breast
　　Shall guard the heart which fondly pulses there
　　That heart the memory of thy love—thy care,
Proudly shall cherish, nor till life shall rest
Cease to extol it, then but to refrain
　　A little time till in that purer land,
　　Far more befitting this all hallowed strain,
Declare thy praises still. There each bright band
Of angels list'ning to the theme, shall swell
　　It into song and each in turn improve
　　Their harps upon an equal theme, and tel!
　　The wondrous story of a mother's love,
—That theme which shall the sweetest songs supply,
As Memory prompts the heavenly minstrelsy !

Solitude.

———

O I do love to wander by the shore !
  And watch the restless waters of the deep,
  As the night winds across Its bosom sweep
Blending their wild complainings with its roar ;
I love to wander through the voiceless wood
  As 'mid its depths the shadowy moonlight creeps
  Where, neath the sentrying stars, tired nature sleeps
And Silence sits enthroned in Solitude.
Such scenes a deep mysterious pleasure bear,
  Waking a slumbering spirit in the breast;
  And from a sleep which knows but little rest
To yield it raptures but experienced there.
Where man may learn—far from the haunts of man,
  In nature's school his own defects to scan.

Music.

———

Come sacred muse naught like thy strains compose
   The longing heart nor there can charm to rest
   Sorrow's lament, Yet O *what* peace it knows
When thy sweet voice steals echoing through the breast.
E'en as a bird which at the break of day
   Called by its mate, joins it and soar away
   Through purest fields of azure, circling round
To some bright glade where cherished fruits abound,
My soul solicitous, at thy behest
   To thy sweet realm joyously wings its flight
   In thy embrace there ravished with delight
Till sweetly soothed it trembles into rest.
—All other joys the passions but control,
   'Tis thou alone hath power to reach the soul.

Licet.

——

Relentless Fate struck by thy venomed dart
  Hope quivering lies,—and palsying dost thou press
Thy icy hand on this despairing heart
  Congealing there all—save its bitterness.
Beneath thy scourge e'en willingly I've stood
  Nor yet complained though sore its lashes fell,
While still hope's star illumined the solitude
  Of disappointment where thou bid me dwell.
But now—and thou would'st bid my heart to quench
  The one sweet light which in this bosom gives
Hope its last ray; and from my breast to wrench
  The dear idea on which alone it lives :
I who have bowed,—nay *loved* thee for this bliss,
Remorseless Fate ! can'st thou not spare me this.

Dolores.

———

Sleep bound me in the lazaret of night.
    Death, wan Despair, sightless Ambition, Lust
    There gathered in contention, 'mid the dust
Of crumbled hopes threw for my heart.—In sight
    It lay sore bleeding, wrenched from its red seat.
Then love, smooth-limbed, white but for heat, there came
With eyes of palpitating fire, a living flame
    That fumed the crimson gouts to vapory heat,
Sweet seeming as the warm breath of desire.
    Death, paling, fled; the noxious crew, dismay
    Struck, livid turned and slank away;
Love healed my heart with kisses of sweet fire
    Burned there *Eternity*, named it her own—
* *   Light 'neath my lids,—ah God! would *Death* had won.

Meditation.

—

In that still hour when the dissolving day
Along the sky fades tranquilly away;
    When o'er the earth the glimmering twilight creeps
    —That drowsiness which falls e'er nature sleeps,
In solitude—naught save the symphony
    Of ocean wakeful, still I seek thy charms,
    Where naught ignoble the glad soul alarms
As it composed resigns itself to thee.
    Silent thou art—thy silence eloquence
Raising the soul to its inherent life,
    Which, casting off its mortal instruments,
Soars far beyond earth's narrow scene of strife,
    And led by thee views that immortal state
    In which it too shall soon participate !

———— —— —— —— ——

NOTE.—Let me here say that the first seven lines of the Sonnet
"The Crucifixion," are imitated from the French of an unknown
author of the seventeenth century. They occur in a little poem enti-
tled " La Mort de Jésus Christ," which was found inscribed upon the
pillars of an old church in Cherbourg, France.

ODDS AND ENDS.

Love and Dignity.

[*An Allegory.*]

It was June : in a vale, as the day was declining,
By a stream which the summer moon studded with light,
Stately Dignity walked, in the silence resigning
His thoughts to those things which most pleasured his sight.

Not far had he gone when he heard a deep sighing,
Which came from a cluster of roses near by,
And great his surprise when among them espying
The little God Cupid, who'd uttered the sigh.

On his arm he reclined, with a rose in his fingers,
From which he was plucking its leaflets away,
While, as a bright star on a cloud's summit lingers,
A tremulous tear on his dark lashes lay.

" And what has disturbed you ? " asked Dignity kindly.
Cupid started and fluttered his wings in dismay,
But feared, in the presence he found himself, blindly
To follow his feelings and scamper away.

He made no reply, simply pointed before him
To an arrow all shattered, the source of his woe,
As he bit those sweet lips for which women adore him,
And patted his bare little leg with his bow.

" Indeed, and is that it ?   Just as I expected.
It would seem you've not done as instructed."   " Tis true."
" Precisely, now had you done as I directed—"
" You would say, I'd not had this misfortune to rue."

" 'This once," Love continued, "good Dignity, spare me,"
Looking up in his face with a suppliant smile,
" Just come here to-morrow at this hour, and hear me
Recount my success with my Beauty meanwhile."

" Most gladly I will ; then good-night,—but *remember*."
" Never fear," Love replied, as he mounted in flight,
With his wings rustling, soft as leaves fanned by a zephyr,
He rose on a moon-beam, and passed out of sight.

Next eve to the spot, ere the Sun had ceased shining,
Came Dignity,—'twas one he long had loved best,—
And there, on a bed of chaste blossoms reclining,
He beheld Beauty, fondling a rose on her breast.

Quick, with rapturing pulsation, his heart beat, but hearing
A sound as of Love's half suppressed voice near by,
He concealed his emotion ; then to her appearing,
He approached, as upon him she smiled graciously.

Love had led her hither ; and now, near her hiding,
'Mid the blossomed-flaked foliage, as Dignity came,
He sped a bright arrowed, flame-tipped, which dividing
His heart, kindled there its wild, exquisite flame.

Thus struck, beside Beauty he fell,—to her pleaded
To draw from his bosom the still flaming dart ;

She, while soothing the wound, saw but Love e'er could
    heal it,
The arrow was buried so deep in his heart!

Then, in flight, Cupid cried, "Dignity, I regret I
Have *missed* you, as now I've no time to wait, for
My quiver is empty; I did not forget you,   .
Believe me; good-night, I am off to get more—

Then his voice, having waked Philomel, 'neath her numbers
Swelling soft in response, melted faintly away,
While the flowers his warm wings had kissed from their
    slumbers,
On the yet wooing sunbeams, spent their sweets wantonly.

—Soon 'twas clear, from the manner of Beauty in pressing
Her hand 'gainst her breast, quickly palpitating,
Love had there sent an arrow;—the rogue when professing
His quiver empty, had his darts 'neath his wing!

Music and Memory.

—

Music once wandering through the heart,
    As daylight died away,
Found Memory sleeping by a tomb
    Fast falling to decay.

Whispering, she touched the slumberer,
    Soft as the pale moon-beam
The folded flower, then passed away
    As vanishes a dream.

Memory awoke, and listening heard
    The rustling wings go by,
Then weeping viewed where she had slept
    And O, how bitterly !

But ah, those tears were sacred,
    And the flowers which there drooped lay,
Beneath their sweet refreshment bloomed
    And beautified decay.

And now no greener spot is there,
    For Memory loves to twine
The richest verdure of the heart
    Around that sacred shrine.

Lines.

Written upon visiting the National Cemetery, Arlington, Va., where are buried the remains of 40,000 Union soldiers, their graves for the most part being marked by a plain white board, many of which bear the simple inscription " Unknown soldier."

To those who "have some friend or brother there."

Ye patriot dead! o'er your sleep of devotion
    Shines the meteor of conquest, while wrapped in death's
        night
Ye rest by that stream—winding down to the ocean,
    Which beheld ye go forth in the pride of your might.

Bright that meteor illumines the shades which enfold ye,
    Reflecting your glory—which brightens its ray—
In the hearts which forever with pride shall behold ye
    Through ages to come, as through years passed away.

And can it then be that "*unknown*" ye are sleeping
    By the scenes of your glory, so valiantly trod;
Can a nation forget that the fruits she is reaping
    Were sown with your lives and refreshed with your blood ?

Ye *are* known : by the hearts which your absence sore
    rending,
  Your valor remembering their anguish consumes ;
By the tears of a Nation which o'er ye descending
    Refresh the sweet flowers which wave o'er your tombs.

Thus not here where the bleak wind in rude lamentation
    Complainingly wanders amid the sad pine
Are ye tombed, but your graves the *warm hearts* of a nation,
    Where evergreen blooming love's memories twine.

No more shall the thunder of battle elate ye ;
  No more shall the trumpet of victory thrill,
Till the last trumpet's sound which forever shall wake ye
    To herald ye onward to victory still

A Vision.

*A fragment of a projected allegorical poem " Love
and Wealth."*

———

" J'etais seul pres des flots pas un nuage auz cieux, sur les mers pas de
voiles, mes yeux plongeaient plus loin que le monde réel "
— *Victor Hugo.*

I had a dream wherein it seemed to me
I stood alone at daybreak, by a sea
Amid whose waves I saw an island rise
—A gem of beauty, 'gainst the azure skies
But little off, and though around me seemed
Night's shadows still, a heavenly brightness beamed
Upon the isle.   From its luxuriant shade
Sloped to the wave a strand, of crystals made ;
—A radiant belt of scintillating light
Which richly sparkled, as faded the night
Along the sea, and as I gazed methought
I was translated to this beauteous spot.
On a hill-side I stood bedecked in blue
Of violets glist'ning 'neath pearly dew,
As the light dawning o'er a flowery rise
With softest shade tinted the lilac skies.
Now gilding the dense foliage of the spot
The risen sun resplendent glory brought,

As stately palms put on their richest hue
And hidden flowers broke upon the view,
Waked by the breeze which, fraught with spicy scent,
With babbling streamlets murmured of content,
While countless songsters decked in varied coats
Greeted each other with their mellow notes.
Of former scenes I seemed to have no thought
—Scarce a remembrance, as entranced I sought
With wandering step each scene with beauty spread)
Of hill and dale in richest verdure clad,
Where floral sweets and fruits luxuriant swayed;)
Now crossing gurgling brooks of purest run
Which sweetly caroled in the wondrous sun ;
Now lost 'mid groves of royal fruits ne'er told
—Entranced, bewildered at this scene of gold.

   *   *   *   *   *   *   *   *

I now beheld a spot more perfect yet,
—If e'er perfection with itself hath met,
It rose from out a plain with gentle slope,
A mount of blossoms to its palm-crowned top,
O'er-ranged with shades with floral wreaths entwined.
Cradling their foliage on the fragrant wind.
Toward this I turned that from its bright ascent
I might survey its summit and extent,
From which—soon reached, I viewed the landscape o'er
On either side ; from further shore to shore,
And thence beheld, o'er many a verdured rise,
The waters stretch to meet the arching skies,
As toward the isle the restless billows rolled,
Their tossing crests enfringed with tints of gold,
From the declining sun, which now to sleep
In wearied splendor sank into the deep.

But the bright moon far up the eastern height
Dispelled the shades of the attendant night,
As thick and fast her silvery arrows flew
Piercing the foliage, while her brightness threw
Light upon all around, and now revealed
A lake before by its rich shades concealed.
In a still vale it slept sentried around
By wooded hills, and sweetly came the sound
Of falling water from the wandering rills
Which left their course among the neighboring hills
To seek its placid bosom.
                              Now reclined
Near the lake's edge exhausted I resigned
Myself to sleep.   I had not thus remained
A moment seemingly but had regained
My strength anew, when suddenly I woke
As on my ear the sound of footsteps broke,
And in the foliage which about me grew
I saw a figure disappear from view.
Breathless I listened, but there came no sound
Save the soft gurgling of the falls beyond
Bright in the moonlight,—then sweet symphonies
Of music rose and died upon the breeze.

Then by the light of the full risen moon
I saw beneath me drawn up from the tide
A little bark from purest coral hewn
Of an exquisite model, from its side
A silver oar, most delicately made,
Drooped in the wave all dripping as it lay,
And tiny footsteps which the sand displayed
Declared its mistress was not far away.

Quick to my feet I sprang for there, O Venus !
What a transporting sight ravished my eyes,
A being not unlike our native genus,
—As far as known from our authorities—
Before me stood, in dress not here the fashion,
A *habitante* of this enchanted clime,
Yet as it proved this most seductive passion,
In her gave place to one far more sublime.

Her feet in ribboned sandals were attired
And—let me see, she wore her dignity
Though to be brief her dress could be admired
For nothing but its strict *economy*.
Liquidly brilliant were her lustrous eyes
Like donna Julia's of Byronic fame,
Reflecting those mysterious sympathies
Love calls to life and else can ne'er proclaim.

Her wealth of hair was rolled into a—
I scarcely know its delicate technique,
Let each one name it what they will, I wist
A goodly number know of what I speak—
And there was born in her sweet eyes a soul
Which she bequeathed me and I lived anew,
And when she sweetly smiled, with full control
That second life to full perfection grew.

She leaned against her little craft which hid
Its coral tint in the delicious glow
Of her soft charms, and as the bright moon shed
Its flood of brilliancy on her fair brow

And in its chrismal shower bathed her sweet form,
Raptured I stood. Then in a voice which spoke
Enchantment, and sweet peace unto the storm
Within my breast, thus she the silence broke :

" Know'st thou this land, or hast thou ne'er before
Explored its sweets—its ever cloudless skies ;
Ne'er known the pleasures of yon further shore
Where now thou hear'st those strains of music rise
Upon the fragrant air ? thence have I come,
Where yonder lights are flashing o'er the scene,
'Tis my abode and the luxurious home
Of mirth and pleasure—I alone its queen."

" Goddess of love," I spoke, approached a pace,
—" And then you know me," quickly she replied,
" Ah beauteous queen, who may behold thy face
Nor know 'tis love and beauty glorified.
This is thy land, fair Venus—this bright sphere
The land of Love and yonder restless sea
The sea of Time ; these symphonies I hear
The joyous sounds of love's glad minstrelsy."

" Well pleased am I to see thee thus display
A knowledge of this land not all possess,
And oft' possessing blindly turn away
To yonder isles adjacent.—Happiness
Foregoing for the gain they madly weigh
Against *this* wealth which man alone can bless,
And for the joy they vainly hope t' attain
Renounce a peace they ne'er can know again."

"Such are the isles of worldly avarice
Where pomp is life and gold man's only aim,
How all excelling this true happiness,
Where life is *love*—love that celestial flame
Which on the height of great Olympus is
That living fire—of heaven the light supreme,
Which daring mortal pillaged from the sky,
Revealing to man the secret of Heaven's joy.

Wealth boasting all no happiness can shed
Where love is not, but is a nothingness ;
A lifeless frame from which the soul is fled ;
A death which hath a form of loveliness,
Like yon pale orb so brilliant yet all dead
Where silence broods in each dark bleak recess :
Radiant it shines all dazzling to behold ;
A sight of beauty but how deathly cold ! "

*   *   *   *

QUAND MÊME.

How shall I paint thy beauties; how relate
Thy virtues? words to compass them so fail;
Thy graces—to the cadence of thy feet,
Make cunning Speech its poverty reveal!
No, this, rude herald, shall not desecrate
The temple of thy form; the graces tell
Of its fair Priestess, matchless!—'twould but be
To subject them t' rude incredulity!

I will not say celestial music's strain
    More richly pours since I have known thy love;
I will not say fair Dian with her train
    Of stars refulgent in their course above
Now brighter shine; and yet each sweet refrain
    Harmonious; yon bright orbs—*all* things now prove
Sources of joy undreamt, and to love yield
Rich springs of beauty ne'er before revealed.

So, as the rising moon with her chaste light
    Doth robe the stars in a new brilliancy,
Raising all sunk in darkness by the night
    To know the glory of her majesty:
Now shall thy love impart a new delight
    To every joy, and life's ambitions be

Exalted to a holier aim, *and yet*,
—Nay, thy sweet eyes rebuke that thought—*forget*.

E'er thus to *sight*, as thought, doth love impart,
  By its mysterious force, higher virtue
Supernal, giving all things to the heart,
  By vision there revealed, an aspect new ;
Clothed in fresh beauty all ; beauty no art
  Hath cunning to resolve, while that we knew
Before as happiness now doth but seem
Like pleasures *waking* buries in a dream !

Thou hast e'en *waked* me ; changed to purest day
The darkness of the past—appearing now
How dark ! as bathed in this new brilliancy
A World of beauty burst upon the view !
And circling round, as doth the earth the sky,
Love doth encompass this creation new,
Of which thou art the Queen, as I would be—
Nay, thou *hast* crowned me Consort unto thee !

Through the soft night, star-studded, of thine eyes,
As in the clouds where silent lightnings play,
Proudly I watch love's sacred fires arise
From the altar thy heart hath built to me,
And there shall love joyously sacrifice
That *self* it hath bound captive, for to thee,
Who hath enthroned its power in my breast,
'Twould consecrate the life thou thus hast blest.

ADIEU.

Adieu but not farewell—ah could we know
The night which waits on that wild word, 'twould seem
Adieu were but a passing cloud—a dream
A momentary darkness but to show
How clear the light succeeding.   Thus we deem
Love e'en may borrow shadows to display,
When drawn the veil, how bright that rarest gem.
In its rich tiara, pure confidence,
Does glitter in its jewelled diadem,
With hope's bright ray—twin meteors which dispense
Within the soul their beams of heavenly day,
Where *angel hands* have rolled the stone away.

Sweet love, adieu, when thou when I am gone
With memory seek'st each love-remembered spot,
Start not if when thou deem'st thyself alone
A presence name thee, thou thou see'st it not.

Its fond, *sad* voice shall breathe to thee of him
Whose heart, from thee, can know no pulse of joy;
And when thou hear'st do thou return love's name
And it shall make thee answer *it is I.*

For as the spirit of the stars invest
   The bosom of the ever wakeful sea,
Though far removed, so shall love's spirit rest
   By its dear shrine, though I am far from thee.

And when thou view'st these warders of the night
With their watch-fires illume the quiet sky,
Bethink thee that those fires changelessly bright,
Image the love this bosom bears for thee. ·

There is a cord deep lying in the heart
Which ne'er responds save to the spirit thrill
Love's absence wakes,—yet O what sad, sweet strains
In that awakening do the bosom fill.

Amid the inner chambers of the soul
   Its sad- --divinely plaintive, harmonies
Echoing steal till 'neath their sweet control
   The longing heart in quiet rapture lies.

Now to thy voice, by gracious Fancy brought,
   Vibrates that cord within this anxious heart,
And wakes a joy with such sweet sorrow fraught
   That joy were less were sorrow to depart.

So, absent, would I wake, in thy sweet breast
   A pulse for each which thrills this heart of mine;
That heart which deems itself, how richly blest
   When e'er it brings one happiness to thine.

Remember me—let not the lamp of thought
   Which lights the shrine that holds my image fail;
And in thy prayers do thou neglect it not
—E'en *there* its beams celestial shall prevail.

Remember *thee !* and wither may *I* fly
  And find thy image from my bosom riven ;
Thy dear idea attends where'er I be,
—E'en in my prayers it leads my thoughts from Heaven.

Yet once again, sweet Love, remember me
  As one whose soul makes thee its one idol ;
And O, how deep that soul's offence must be
If 'tis a crime on earth to love too well.

Good-night, farewell ; *farewell*, ah, how doth love
  Against that word, next feared to *death*, rebel ;
Nay, *more* than death *that* to this heart should prove,
And death thrice sweet the hour that brings *farewell*.

IN MEMORIAM.

  I stood alone on the pebbled beach
  As the moon rose over the sea,
  And the doleful break of the restless waves
  Brought sad memories to me.

  I saw o'er the path which the moon-beams traced
  A ship pass into the night :
  Though it hurried by ere I'd viewed it well,
  I can never forget that sight.

  E'en thus, I thought, on life's path appear
  Sweet faces a moment seen,
  Then dead to us :—a grave in the heart
  Which memory keeps ever green.

The Moon.

————

Thou orb sublime ! that from the boundless sky
   Dost move the sombre shadows of the night,
To flood the world in mellow brilliancy,
   That calmly soothes yet ravishes the sight.

Now as thy beams invade my chamber's gloom
   And slowly wake the slumbering shadows there,
What drear abodes of misery they illume
   Where all is fled save anguish and despair ;

What thoughts disturb the lonely convict's heart,
   As now he views thee from his ironed cell,
Of childhood's scenes—of cherished hopes depart,
   Which he remembers—ah, too sadly well.

He feels thy beams, which now his prison search,
   Look on a scene which memory weeps to trace :
—A lowly grave behind the village church
   Of her who sank beneath a child's disgrace.

What great variety of scenes untold
   Hast thou beheld—what mighty empires sway,
As through unnumbered ages thou hast rolled
   As now thou roll'st unchanged,—yet where are they ;

Where now is haughty Babylonia's might
  Which madly dared Omnipotence deride?
—For thou *hast* too illumined her guilty site
  As now the plain which sepulchres her pride.

So shall thy beams before another sun
  Look on the walls of crumbling Pompeii,
And from the heights of silent Lebanon
  Flood the still waves of holy Galilee.

Infinite theme,—O thrice infinite God!
  Whose hand directs e'en as his hand hath made,
Who shall presume to limit his abode
  Or *count* the wonders of his works displayed?

—Adieu sweet moon, fast fading from the sight,
Low in the west,—Yet once again good night.

Church Litany.

(*Versified.*)

O God the King of Heaven thou !
Before thy throne we sinners bow,
Our sins with mercy look upon
For Jesu's sake thine only Son.

O God the Son, Redeemer we
Unworthy sinners look to thee ;
Thy mercy—thou once sorrow knew,
To us most miserable show.

O God, Great Spirit, Holy One !
Proceeding from the Father Son,
In prayer our souls we lift to Thee
To us a strong defender be.

O Father, Son, and Spirit three
One blest and glorious Trinity !
Look down in mercy as we bend,
To us thy timely succor lend.

Remember not, O Gracious God!
Our paths nor those our fathers trod,
Spare us, by thy most precious blood;
O, spare us from thy vengeful flood.

From evil mischief and all sin;
From Satan's crafts without, within;
From thy just wrath, eternal night
Protect us by thy Mercy's might.

By Thy Holy Incarnation;
Thy baptism, fast, temptation;
By Thy memory of Thy birth;
By Thy agony of earth;

By Thy pain, Thy bloody sweat;
By Thy cross—Thy Passion, death;
By Thy dread sepulchral sleep;
By Thy love—Thy mercy deep.

By Thy Resurrection shown;
Thy Ascension to Thy Throne;
By Thy Holy Spirit's sway,
O Christ, deliver us, we pray.

When tossed upon life's troubled sea;
In all the world's prosperity;
In death's dark hour—the Judgment Day.
O Christ! deliver us, we pray.

That it may please Thee in Thy love
Our Sovereign's heart to wisdom move ;
May she in Jesu's strength put on
Affiance have in Thee alone.

Thou Heaven's enthroned whose blood was shed
That we might live though Thou wert dead,
Suffer us not in life's last breath
To sink to an eternal death.

O Lamb of God ! how dark the night,
Which Thine own love hath made so bright ;
Through life, in death be thou the way
Which leads us to eternal day.

Sweet Flower.

"Sweet flower and must thy beauty fade
 Though born but yesterday ;
Scarce one short day of life, and now
 Thou hasten'st to decay ? "

" True, brief is my abiding here "
 Replied the flower, " and yet
If Earth be sweeter for my life
 I know not of regret."

To My Bird.

———

Who fashioned thy exquisite symmetry
  Thou little elf of song; thou paragon
  Of grace, what wondrous cunning artisan
The fabric wove of thy chaste livery?

What hand the delicate machinery cast
  Which thus thy wings so marvelously propel;
Who in thy tiny frame its forces placed,
  And made them thus obedient to thy will?

What hast thou in that little throat of thine
  Which trills such notes of dulcet purity;
Who taught thee thus in minstrelsy divine
  To pour thy song in rhythmic harmony?

Perchance it was, in thine own native shades,
  The purling brook, the voices of the woods,
Where now thy fellows in the flowery glades
  Awake to song the island solitudes.

But these *thou* ne'er hast known,—then 'twas thy sire
   Tuned thy sweet voice?—nay, loud thy numbers tell,
In praises rising softly, sweetly higher,
   'Twas nature's God that fashioned thee so well.

Would I could tell thee how I love thy song;
   How dear to me, my pretty one, thou art:
Why dost thou fly me?—I but fondly long
   With kindliest hand to lay thee to my heart.

How happily would'st thou lie upon this breast
   Did'st thou but know how warms my heart to thee,
Yet nestling there, in thy sweet eyes' unrest
   Pained I behold thou 'dst gladly fly from me.

Thou can'st not understand by words I know,
   But love hath many voices and for thee
Nature has surely purposed one, and so
   I am content that Time should teach it me.

A Fragment.

—–

In death thou sleep'st, thrice blest immunity !
Life's ills to change for immortality ;
A stranger here, thy soul in glad release
Has sought the regions of eternal peace.
What though thy dust supports the lowly sod
—-Earth's final task,—thy soul is with thy God ;
Though cold and dark may seem thy earthly bed,
It holds but dust, thy ransomed spirit fled
To those bright shores where, welcomed by the bless'd,
It knows the fullness of its Saviour's rest.
Herein where death aspires to victory,
It gives the soul a perfect liberty —
The grave, which e'er to crush the soul has striven,
Proving the portal to the courts of heaven.
Spring comes again, but what to thee is spring?
Thou may'st not hear the birds which o'er thee sing,
Nor see the flowers which come from thy decay
Bedeck thy tomb, and thus their debt repay.
The sentrying pines sigh in the night wind's gust,
Spreading their roots to mingle with thy dust,
Seeming to chant thy slumber's lullaby,
Yet wherefore this ? thou sleep'st unwakingly,
Until the morning of the resurrection break,
When death itself shall sleep, no more to wake !

A Thought.

I watched a rose in Autumn drop away,
  Its crimson richness leaf by leaflet fade,
And sadly gazing thought may thus decay
  Such beauty bear to its unwholesome shade?

I sought in vain the glisten of the dew
  Upon the blossoms, on the verdured lawn :
Shivering the flowers their leaflets closer drew
  'Neath the chill breath of the October dawn.

The spirit of the flower, the fire, methought,
  Which kindles in the dew thus fled must pass
To some bright sphere, and straight my Fancy sought
  To trace a spot worthy such loveliness.

To Phosphor‡ floating in her sea of light,
  An isle of glory ; to the enchanted sphere
Arched by the Iris ; to each star its flight
  Did fancy wing—successless voyager !

*   *   *   *   *   *   *

‡ The Morning Star.

I stood amid a scene of festal joy
   Dazzlingly bright, sweet music wooed the air,
And cradled in its soft embrace Beauty
   Which trembled to behold itself so fair.

Then love exulting cried : " that fit repose
   By Fancy sought 'e'en here all radiant view :
In Beauty's cheek immortal blooms the rose ;
   In Beauty's eyes the fires born in the dew ! "

LOVE IN ABSENCE.

En el amor la auscencia es como el aire, que apaga el fuego chico e
enciende el grande. —Spanish proverb.

A little fire
Does soon expire
'Neath the wind's agitation,
While 'neath the same
A greater flame
Becomes a conflagration.

And so in love
Does absence prove
—A little fire o'erturning ;
But when the breast
Love's flames *invest*
It sets them wildly burning.

Lines in an Album.

As oft' beneath the churchyard's quiet shade
  We wander musing at the close of day,
And mark the sadd'ning records telling there
Of fondest friendships which have passed away :
So in life's evening when thine eyes shall stray
Amid these pages, to thy memory dear,
Know thou this *leaf* rests *in memoriam*
To friendship's tribute which I offer *here*.

THE SAME.

Far in the aftertime when years have fled
And thou dost weep o'er cherished friendships dead,
O may thy tears refresh that sacred spot
Where fading droops the sweet "forget-me-not."

THE SAME.

Spotless this page where now my verse I place
  —The *purer* record of thy life e'en thus :
Would that as *here Friendship* I fondly trace,
  I *there* might grave *Unfading happiness*.

THE SAME.

Dear girl of all the darling flowers
    That bloom along the way,
Beneath thy love which makes their life
    Thine eyes which make their day,
Turn in some moments to regard
    In this secluded spot
The *leaf* I offer friendship here
    From the forget-me-not.

THE SAME.

When nature wakes or slumbers;
When distant far from thee,
Among remembered numbers
Ne m'oubliez pas, je prie.

— •••

JMITATED FROM THE FRENCH.

If thou would'st love one whom I love,
    Thyself must thou adore,
How deeply, would that I might prove
    To thee,—love could no more.

Love to the Mirror

Since all my darts in vain assail her breast,
  Show thou to her the charms for which I sigh,
That wooed thy beauty she entranced may gaze
  And, like Narcissus, self-enamored die.

Epigrams.

His last debt he has paid—poor Clark 's no more—
Last debt : pray when did he pay one before ?

Melissa says she hates a flatterer—
            'twould seem,
Then I am wrong in charging her
            with *self-esteem !*

FRIENDSHIP.

.How sweet to find the heart by Friendship proved,
Through years of absence still remain unmoved;
To find the shades of changeful years have ne'er
Shadowed the image love enshrined there.

Thus o'er the ever widening stream of Time;
From on the shore of some far distant clime,
How sweet to hear those voices loved before,
Call on our name from off the further shore.

And oh how sweet when friendships all have flown,
To find one heart we still can call our own:
'Tis sure the Angels here the stone unroll,
So heavenly bright the beams which flood the soul.

When First J Met Thee.

When first J met thee I had thought
  Love from my heart his flight had ta'en;
Nor dreamed he there had hidden aught
  To tempt him to return again.

But ah ! thy starry eyes illumed
  My heart's inmost recesses, where
The sweetest flowers profusely bloomed
  Which I had never dreamt were there.

Love's choicest sweets—they ne'er had known
  The light of other eyes than thine;
With which chaste offerings all thine own,
  He bids me yield this heart of mine.

For now a little despot he,
  'Mid richest blooms, there reigns supreme,
And wakes to song sweet *Poesie*,
  Who joyous syllables thy name.

Then fairest one, that I may live
  To know these sweets revealed by thee,
Return the heart I freely give,
  And yield thine own in turn to me.

Song.

———

Sweet bird of spring, I greet thee
Though thou sorrow bring'st to me,
As glad as are the numbers
Of thy sweet minstrelsy ;
Thy presence wakes sad memories
Of the love I lost with thee,
Till I scarce can bear the anguish
Of the thoughts that rise in me.

With thee, the flowers gray Autumn
Laid in Earth's snow-white breast
Return, but he may ne'er come back
Whom *I* laid there to rest ;
And so, e'en to thy happy song—
Too brief for joy before, .
Must sorrow's voice within my heart
Lament forevermore.

To Félise.

———

I love to look into thine eyes,
The windows of the soul,
Where scintillate in lettered light
Sweet truths words ne'er control.

I love to look into thine eyes
—Sweet springs which sparkling o'er
Life's arid plain, a verdure bring
There never known before.

I love to look into thine eyes,
Where virtues mirrored are;
Virtues which modesty would hide
By truth revealed there.

ERRATA TYPOGRAPHICA :—

Page	Line	No. of word	Reads	Should be
6	28	5	languid	liquid
7	6	5	freshing	fresh*en*ing
14	1	5	staggering	struggling
16	18	2	wonder*s*	*Wonder*
19	19	8	vision	vision*s.*
24	29	3	th*r*ough	though
25	3	5	that	the*n*
26	1	6	breast	brea h
26	13	3	*of*	*a hyphen.*
27	4	6	was	*is*
30	7	last	side*s*	side.
34	16	5	too	*to*
34	30	2	presse*d*	presse*s*

For lines 6 to 10, division vii, page 27, please substitute the following :

Till winding 'twixt a chasmed rock, it seemed
To seek repose 'neath the o'ershadowing height,—
Whose frowning brow repelled the soft moonlight-
As some great serpent drags its weary length
Into the darkness of its cavern-strength !